Curious George

Little Book of Curiosity

PEOPLE AND PLACES

Illustrated in the style of H. A. Rey by Greg Paprocki

Houghton Mifflin Harcourt Publishing Company

Boston   New York

www.hmhbooks.com
www.curiousgeorge.com

The text of this book is set in New Century Schoolbook.
The illustrations are watercolor, pencil, and charcoal.

Illustrated by Greg Paprocki

ISBN 978-0-544-05284-0

Manufactured in China

LEO 10 9 8 7 6 5 4 3 2

4500412425

This is George.

He is a good little monkey
and always very curious.

Let's see what George is curious about today...

sister

brother

father

mother

grandparents

friend

Family

uncle

aunt

friend

cousins

pet

friends

Your Neighborhood

school

statue

playground

streetlights

traffic light

street sign

bushes

sidewalk

crosswalk

crossing guard

lamppost

truck

sprinkler

street

leaves

mailbox

trees

fire hydrant

neighbors

movie theater

flag

bus

STORE

BUS STOP

POLICE

FIRE HOUSE

pay phone

flowers

car

fire truck

Jobs

librarian

teacher

police officer

astronaut

firefighters

farmer

lifeguard

carpenter

nurse

scientist

magician

rock star

doctor

janitor

dancer

fisherman

baker

soldier

pilot

veterinarian

store clerk

writer

artist

athlete

hairdresser

letter carrier

Home Sweet Home

house

tree house

igloo

castle

skyscraper

hut

cabin

trailer

pueblo

houseboat

birdhouse

apartment

Where's George?

steak

chicken

cheese

cash register

shopping cart

bread

EXIT

swings

monkey bars

kite

kickball

merry-go-round

baseball bat

baseball glove

baseball

Parts of the Body

hair

head

ears

teeth

arms

fingers

elbow

hands

eyes

nose

mouth

legs

back

bottom

belly

knees

toes

feet

Emotions Sometimes I feel...

surprised

scared

sad

sleepy

angry

happy

Farm Animals and Sounds

farmhouse

field

cat

meow

cock-a-doodle-doo

rooster

fence

baaaa

sheep

cluck
cluck

oink

peep

chicken

pigs

chick

sun

volcano

mountains

valley

river

lake

forest

Bath Time

mirror

towel

toothbrush
toothpaste

shampoo

soap

bathrobe

sink

rubber
duckie

slippers

comb

hairbrush

tub

toilet

clothes
hamper

Bedtime

curtains

poster

clock

bed

lamp

pajamas

night-light

blanket

teddy bear

bedtime story

friends

blocks

toys

What will George be curious about tomorrow?